MONK CAMPS OUT

story and pictures by EMILY ARNOLD McCULLY

Arthur A. Levine Books An Imprint of Scholastic Press

Monk decided it was the perfect night
for his first camp-out.

He'll be back
before we know it.

First, Monk had to make a tent.

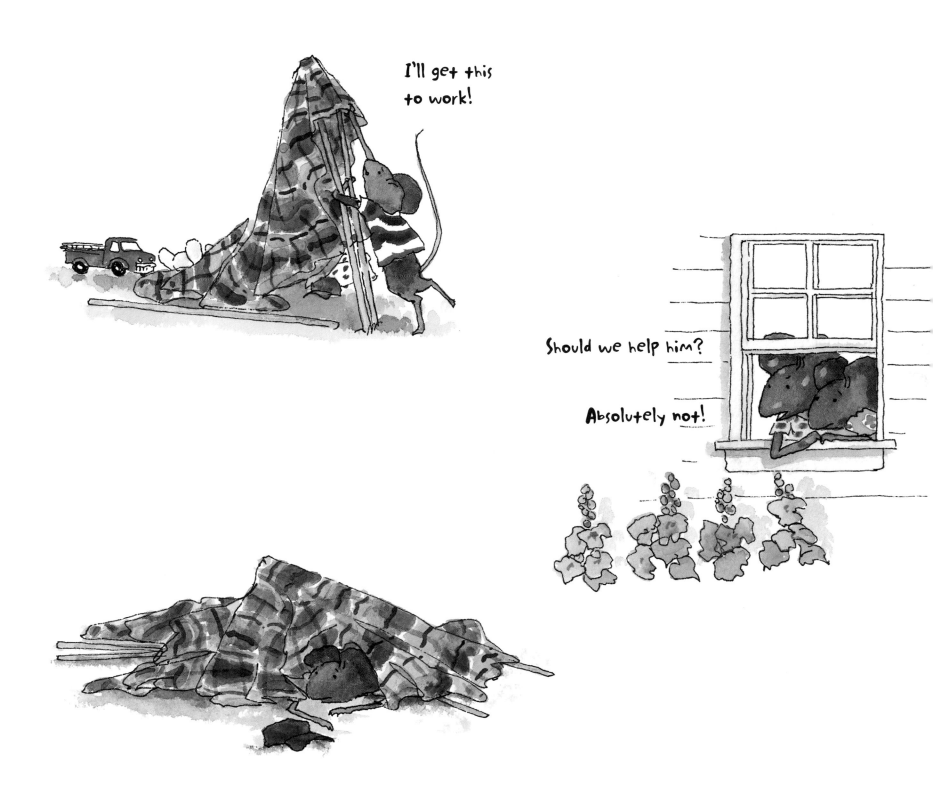

They only helped a little.

Of course, nobody answered.

Dinner was quiet.

The sun went down.
Monk watched shadows creep.
The kitchen light went out.
The living room light went on.

Who could sleep with all that quiet?

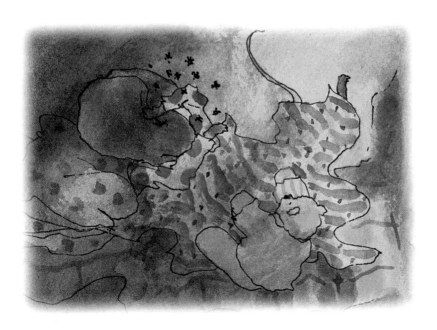

The door flew open.

We have to give him
a good-night hug!

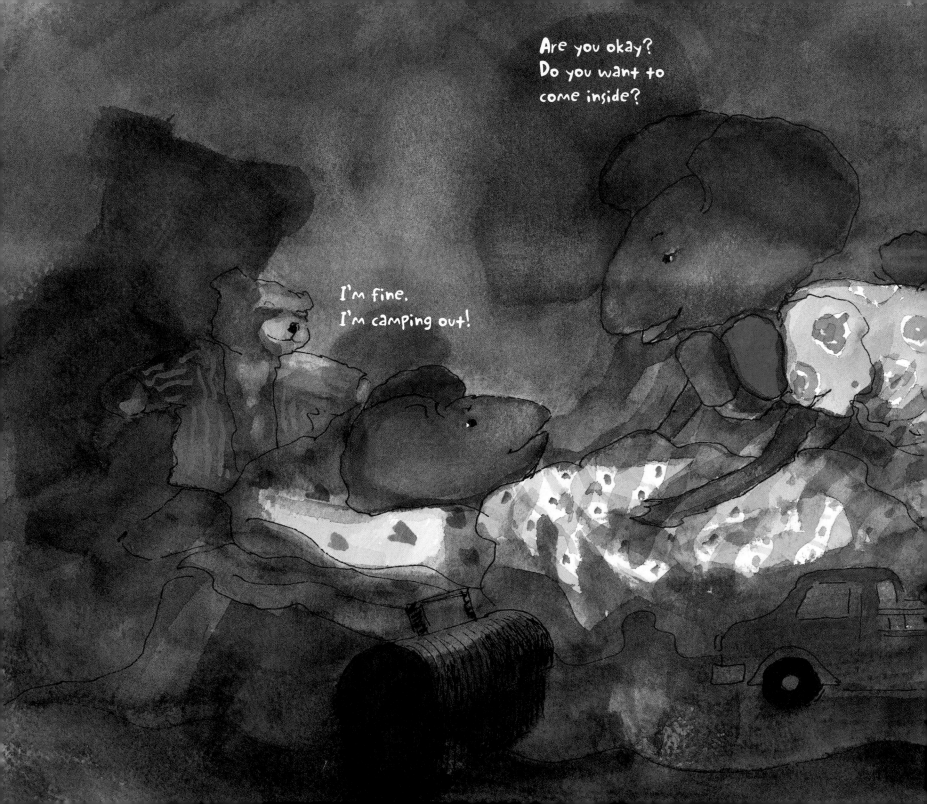

They were proud of Monk.

He's very brave.

We'll just stay up until
he decides to come in.

Later that night, Monk woke up!

Where am I?

Where's my mitt?

Dad?

Quiet as mice, they peeked inside.

We'll just sleep out here and keep him company.

Mom's chair was still warm.

Good morning!

Where is everybody?

Mom! Dad!

Monk!

Zzzzzzz.

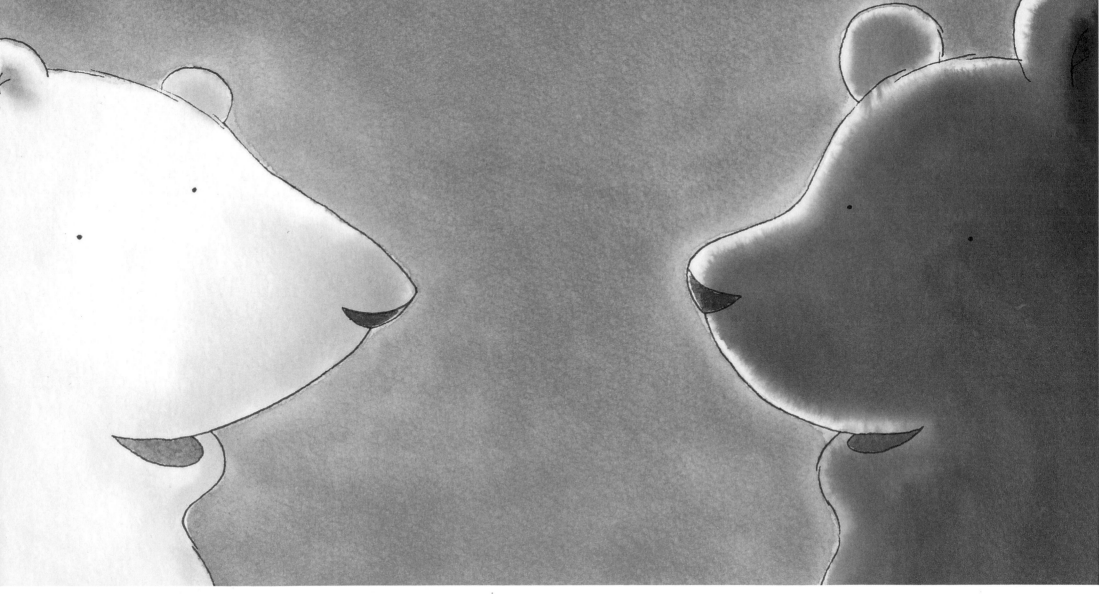

A Secret Promise

BY CRISTINA CRENGUTA DOCAN
ILLUSTRATED BY BORIS JOH PASSACANTANDO

BEAUTIFULBOOKS

First published 2006.

Beautiful Books Limited
117 Sugden Road
London SW11 5ED

www.beautiful-books.co.uk

ISBN 1905636016/9781905636013

9 8 7 6 5 4 3 2 1

Text ©Cristina Crenguta Docan 2006
Illustrations ©Boris Joh Passacantando 2006
Design by Ian Roberts
Production by nlAtelier
Printed in Italy by Graphicom

For Raluca, Naghisa and Yuki-Cookie,
the most amazing moon-like golden drops on the earth.

Cristina

To Cinzia with all my love
to my parents
to Cristina
to Simon and Tamsin with special gratitude
and to the two little bears

Boris

Far, far away, on the wooded slope of a mountain, lives the Little Brown Bear.

He is the most beloved son of the forest.
He is a very happy bear.

Far, far away, on a notched iceberg torn off from a huge glacier, lives the Little White Bear.

He is the most beloved son of the North Pole. He doesn't have a worry in the world.

The Little Brown Bear is a cheerful fellow.
At dawn, all the animals in the wood wait
impatiently for the little cub to wake up.
It is only then, when he joyfully bursts into
peals of laughter, that the day really begins.

The Little White Bear lives in a spotless white land, which seems to have no end and no beginning. He was born at the end of the polar winter. He loves to explore, either sitting on his father's strong back or following closely behind him.

From sunrise to sunset,
the Little Brown Bear is restless.
He clambers on his mother's back to see the world. He rolls down
the silky grass hill, filled with joy. And when no-one is around,
feeling curious, he digs up anthills. The tiny
creatures carry huge pieces of luggage.
"*Where do they hide them?*" he wonders.

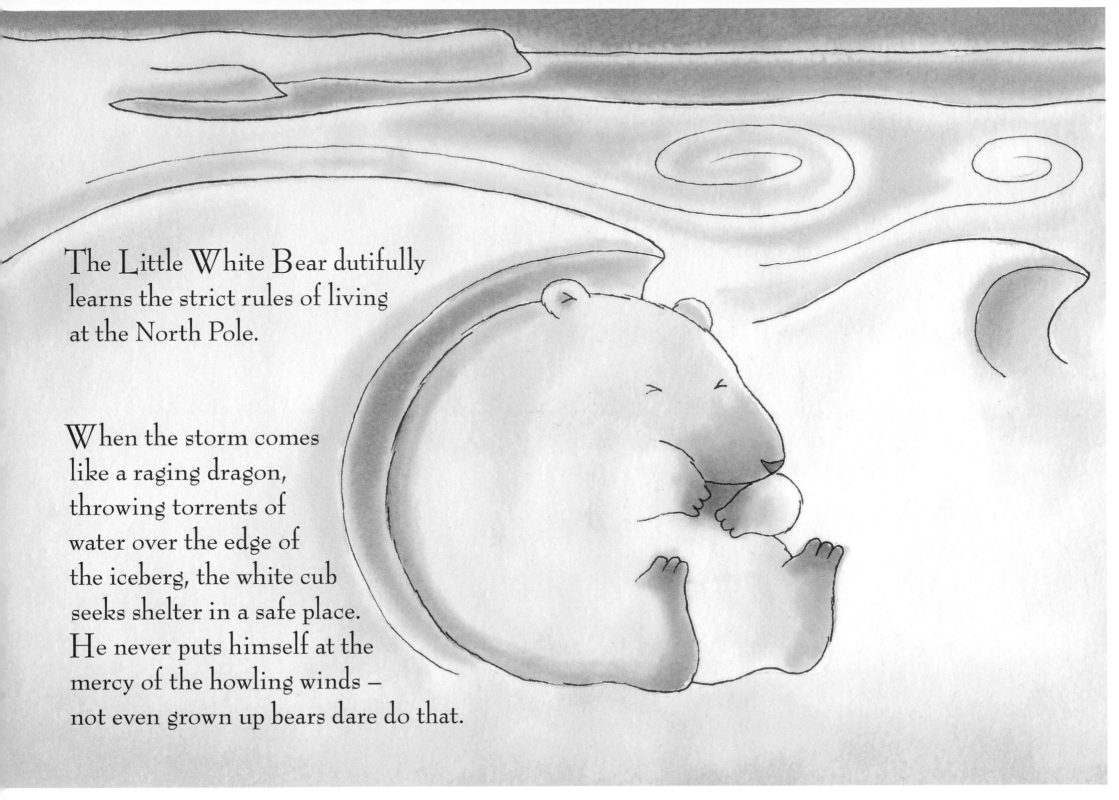

The Little White Bear dutifully learns the strict rules of living at the North Pole.

When the storm comes like a raging dragon, throwing torrents of water over the edge of the iceberg, the white cub seeks shelter in a safe place. He never puts himself at the mercy of the howling winds — not even grown up bears dare do that.

Though he is no
taller than a Tom Thumb, the brown
cub wants to prove he is ready to face the
challenges of life. Watched by his friends,
the cheeky squirrels and the grumpy badgers,
the Little Brown Bear climbs a small ash
tree. But when he reaches the top, he suddenly
feels scared and has to call out for help!

When the weather is kind,
the white cub loves to spin
around on the ice, playing
with the loveable old seals
who are almost deaf. They
caress him with sweet talk
and beg him over and over
again to sing the sad song they
taught him about the starry polar night.

The Little Brown Bear is always busy. But after lunch, he feels terribly tired, his tummy stuffed full after thrusting his nose deeply in a bilberry bush. Just before falling asleep, he growls with satisfaction: *"Isn't this the most beautiful place on earth?"*

At sunset, the white mother bear breaks holes in the thin ice.
The Little White Bear loves to watch the dance of the little fish snatched
up by his mother. As happy as can be, he slides about on the bright snow,
shrieking with joy. *"Hurrah-ah-ah!"* his voice echoes far away.
"Isn't this the most beautiful place on earth?"

From time to time, the Little White Bear
and the Little Brown Bear come across each other in dreams.

They run shoulder to shoulder on endless white lands, wander through shady woods and climb beautiful mountains.

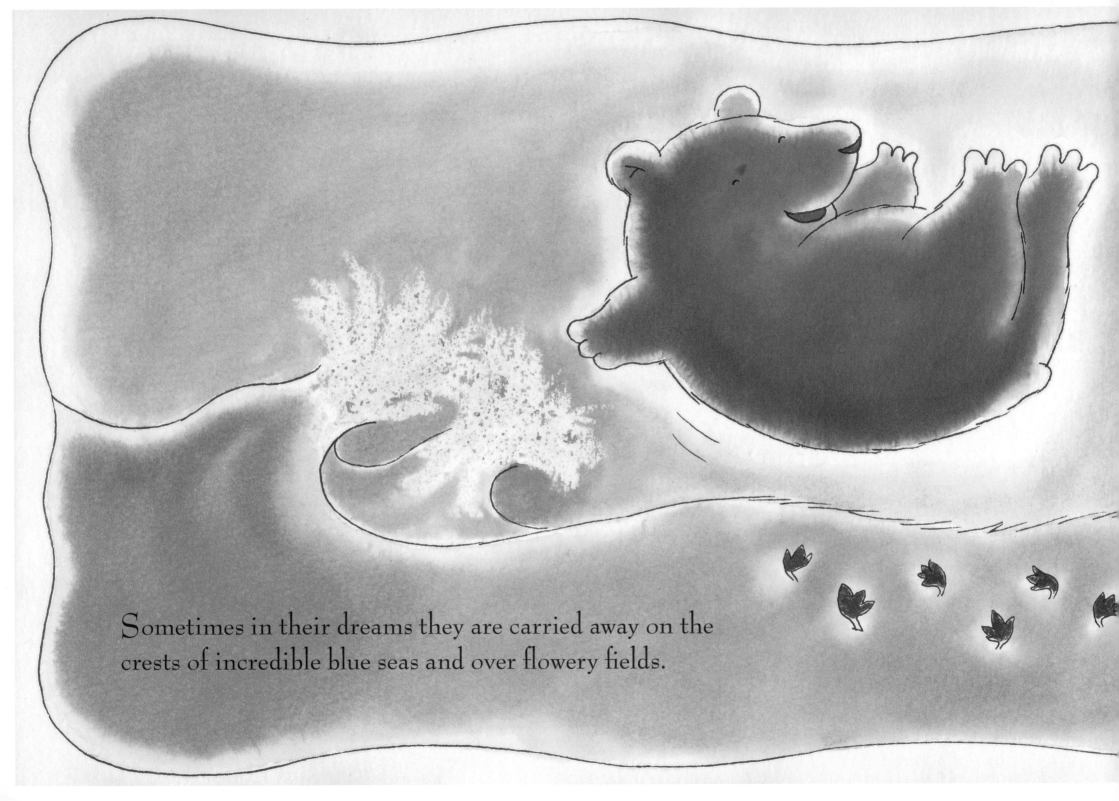

Sometimes in their dreams they are carried away on the crests of incredible blue seas and over flowery fields.

They fly over dry, golden deserts and across amazing, rushing rivers.

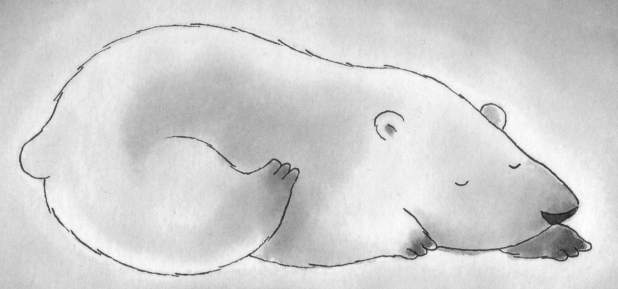

Does this surprise you?

Don't you know that all bears dream like this when they are small?
Then one day they grow up, and their dreams are forgotten, left behind
in the magic world of childhood.

But the Little White Bear and the Little Brown Bear both know what they must do: when they grow up, they promise to follow their dreams. They will both set out to discover all that the world has to offer.

It's a secret promise that they want to share just with you.
And do you know what? You can do it too.

You can follow your dreams.

I can already imagine it: shoulder to shoulder, the Little White Bear, the Little Brown Bear, and you, all you brave bears and children!

The End

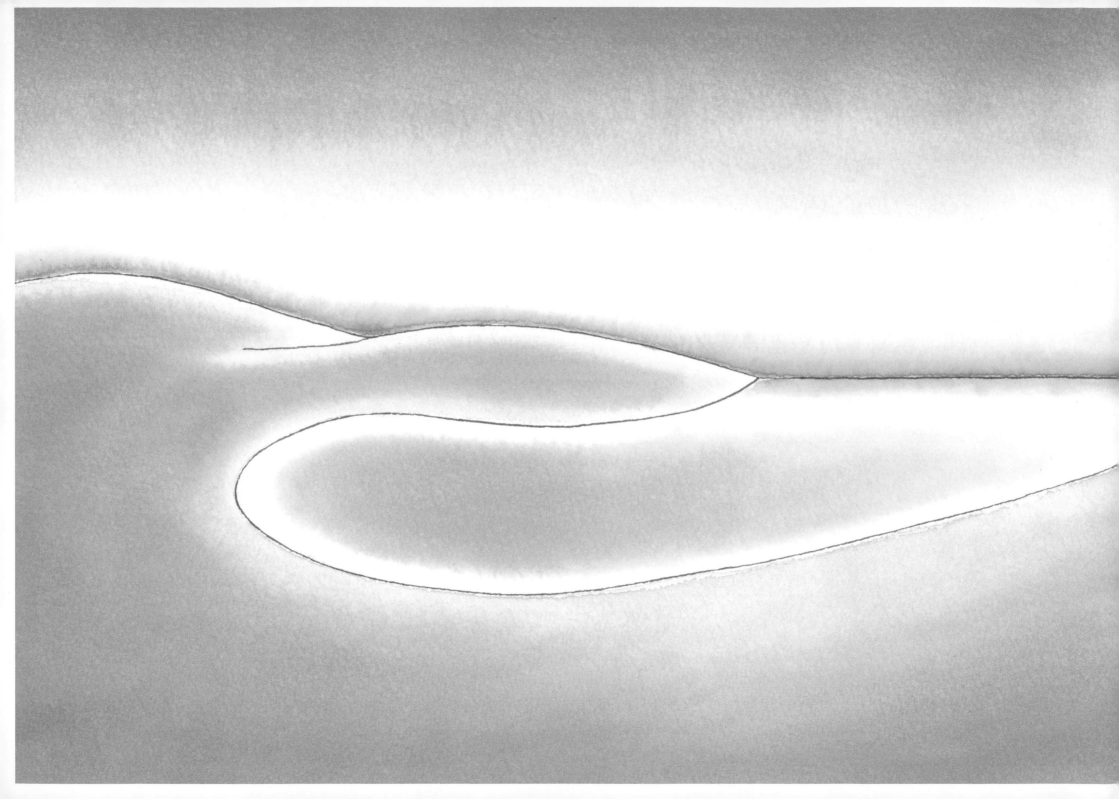